# DEATH REEL

IS THERE MORE BEYOND THE BIG
SCREENS OF FATE?

# KIMBERLY KINNAMAN

ISBN: 979-8-9901496-0-1  (paperback)

ISBN: 979-8-9901496-1-8  (e-book)

Library of Congress Control Number: 2024905069

This book is a work of fiction. All references to names, historical events, characters, beliefs, organizations, incidents, and places are products of the author's imagination or are used fictitiously.

Cover Design by Books and Moods

Printed by Kimberly Kinnaman Portland OR, United States of America

First printing edition, 2024

To every one of my family and friends who said,<br>
"Kill me in your book!"

# OMNIST

A person who does not claim any one belief but finds truth in them all.

# TRIGGER WARNING

Contains graphic depictions of suicide, death, dismemberment, abortion, and sexual assault.

# FOREWORD

In this world, your death and afterlife are recovered and played in theatres around the globe. Death-reels are recordings of an individual's personal belief systems and may not accurately portray the religion those individuals have practiced in life. No two people will imagine the exact same things!

I live in a constant state of existential dread, welcome to my mind.

# CHAPTER ONE

"You have to believe it. I mean, really, deep down in your guts, no doubt in your mind, believe it! Or it's not gonna stick. That's the problem with knowing; when you know, you can't fool yourself anymore. Don't go to the theatres... if you want an afterlife. Because once you know, there's no going back."

When you die, the last thoughts you have are recorded. These death-reels are played at local theatres. In this small town, there are two theatres running, one named *Heaven* and one named *Hell*. Each has an allure that keeps people coming back; *Heaven* is, well, heavenly, while *Hell's* aesthetic is dark and mysterious. Business at the theatres has slowed down over the years as people have started to accept that the long-promised afterlife appears to be a figment of their imaginations. As soon as the theatre became mainstream, some death-reels started showing the deceased sitting in an empty theatre watching a blank production; after all, one of the greatest fears in life is being forgotten. Occasionally, someone who hadn't stepped foot in a theatre would pass and their reel would be the most vivid, wild ride. Theatres would be packed with people who would ooh and aww, wishing that their imaginations would be as great, when they met their end.

Adrien could remember the warning her father had given her a million times, but this was different; she couldn't find any reason to stay away from the theatres today. Her father's showing was being featured in *Hell*, which came as a surprise to the whole family. She needed to know what had happened to him. Had he been able to fool himself, or was his screen going to be blank? Seeing as they were in *Hell*, a place for eternal damnation, nightmares, judgment, conspiracy theories, suicide, and generally unpleasant deaths - it concerned her greatly not knowing exactly what to expect.

How could he condemn himself to such a fate when he was the voice of reason? A man who had spent his life helping others create their own afterlife. He had run an outreach program for wayward souls, people who needed something to believe in since the revelation that the idea of an afterlife, as agreed upon by the general public, was purely make-believe. In title, he was a Death Curator, a creator of imagination, an affirmer of beliefs, and a man who served his fellow man until the day he died. His job was especially important for those who couldn't go back to the churches since they chose knowledge over God. When someone attended a death reel, even if it was of their loved ones, they were ex-communicated. The church's reasoning was that if God had wanted them to know about the afterlife, he would've taught them himself. If you went to the theatres, you were turning your back away from religion and toward the lying word of man.

The conspiracy theories that followed the opening of the theatres were grandiose and numerous. Everything from it's all made up by the government to control the masses, to the interference of Satanic powers, or Alien technology that abducts our loved ones, leaving the films to trick you into believing they died of natural causes. Natural being old age, sickness, accidents, murder, or suicide. As with all conspiracy theories, this has spurred some amazing death-reels, starring each scenario with intricate details changing only based upon the individual's personal beliefs. Entertaining as it was to watch aliens abduct spirits from dead bodies, it was morbid to know that the person starring in the show was indeed, and without a doubt, dead.

She walked into the theatre taking note of the red and black patterned carpet, creating the illusion that the theatre's interior matched its namesake. The walls were matte black with red neon lights strung between viewing houses. Adrien's breath caught in her throat as the echo of her quickening heartbeat filled the empty hall, not another soul in sight. No one had seen this morning's death-reels, the theatre reserves first showings for families and friends, those mourning their loved ones. Her father had passed in his sleep two nights ago, a peaceful way to go, meaning his reel would be unaffected by his death. She coaxed her feet to continue forward. Crossing the threshold, she found her family sitting in the front row. While "Don't go to the theatres" played repeatedly in her head, she perched on the seat unable to settle her nerves... The smell of stale popcorn hung in the air, making her wonder, *what kind of sick freaks would come to the death-reels and be able to eat knowing what they were about to watch.*

"Ladies and Gentlemen, welcome to the Death Reel of Benjamin Morgan Burnum, loving husband and father of three..." The rest of the introduction was his obituary. Who needed the newspaper anymore when your loved one's death was broadcast on the big screen? Sometimes, in the case of a particularly good death-reel, it could reach theatres worldwide. As the introduction trailed off, the lights dimmed in the theatre, and Adrien leaned into her chair needing the extra support as she questioned her choice coming today. "Don't go to the theatres." Maybe his beliefs had landed him in a tortured afterlife. What if she could learn from his death-reel how to give herself a better one? No reason she could configure to excuse her presence today mattered. She knew why she chose to come to the theatres today: to see him one last time.

She could feel the silence in the way her breath caught in her chest, not daring to release a molecule of air for fear of missing something important. In the dark, Adrien's hand tightened around her mother's; the tears Adrien had been holding back all day were fresh on her cheeks as a familiar face appeared on the big screen. Neither could look away. This was too important. They needed to know why this reel was showing in *Hell*. The image on the screen was of her father's last moments, sleeping in bed, when a new character appeared. The new man reached out his hand and pulled the spirit from her father's body.

"That's strange, I didn't think I would create a god," Ben said.

"I'm not a god, I'm the narrator. I'm here to guide you through your afterlife," the stranger said.

"Lead the way, I've been building this my entire life. I can't wait to see what my imagination came up with!" The narrator lead Ben away from his sleeping body, through a door into a bright white room. The room, though void of inhabitants, was remarkable, blindingly bright, yet invitingly warm. Once inside, the narrator began to speak.

"I have brought you to this place of nothingness, the place where you feel you belong after life. This is the place that all the living fear, the reason for Gods, for religions, for belief, and hope. This is a place you claim will be your end, but not until you've chosen a good story to leave behind for those you love."

"Nothing never looked so good. Not what I imagined, but not a disappointment. At least I'll get a good tan in the afterlife." Ben chuckled at his own joke, but the narrator was unamused.

"You will be given the chance to choose." Several doors appeared before them, much like the theatre's halls. "You will choose a door. Each is labeled, not with a name, but with an adventure that you have curated for yourself. Only after you have explored, will you know what truly lies beyond the grave."

Ben walked down the theatre-esque hall of doors, all floating in the nothingness, each with a different label.

"Adventure", "Heaven", "Hell", "Reincarnation", and at the end of the hall he found a door he didn't remember curating, labeled "Unknown". He stopped. He looked equally surprised and amused at this door. What wonders lie beyond? Would it be a Russian roulette of all the afterlives he had curated throughout the years, or would it be something entirely different? Was he willing to go through this door, not knowing what to expect, but knowing full well that it was the last thing he would ever do? Yes. He grasped the knob, turned it, and all the other doors disappeared as he pulled the unknown wide open.

# CHAPTER TWO

Adrien's head was spinning the moment she stepped out of the theatre; she felt much like the reels unwinding stories of the departed. Later that night, standing in her kitchen washing dinner dishes, she thought about the hall of doors and the door he'd chosen. Was there still room for surprise in the afterlife? No wonder her father's death-reel had made it into *Hell:* all conspiracy theories ended up there. It stopped the public from believing in more beyond the big screens of fate. The consensus was if everyone knew what was coming, then it would alleviate some of the fear and unease around death. The world had become apathetic, accepting their fate to be pre-determined by their imagination, all except for a few religious outliers and those they'd convinced to follow them.

After stepping through that door, her life could never be the same. She programmed her coffee pot to brew at 6 am. In the morning, she would head out to the theatres again.

This morning, she wasn't going back to her father's reel. She was looking for answers to the questions that yesterday's showing had borne in her. She walked into *Hell* and read the obituary posters: Allen King - Religious Hell of Brimstone and Fire, Stephanie Madrigal - Personal Hell of Lobsters attacking while she isn't wearing shoes, Josie Pallouchi - Sitting in a theatre watching her death-reel: a compilation of every mistake she had ever made, and James Lander - Losing his family. Each reel was capped at 3 hours, although some could be an all-day ordeal. The theatres shorten them unless they're deemed worthy of watching; pre-screeners plan intermissions for the longer death-reels. Her father's reel had been 5 hours long, and every second of it was worth the watch. This was reaffirmed by the continued airtime of 5 hours today when his viewing was open to the public.

Heading to her viewing house, she felt a familiar tug in her midsection. Her stomach let out a groan of dissatisfaction; she'd forgotten breakfast in her hurry. Coffee alone wasn't enough to nourish the body. Reluctantly, she turned towards the popcorn counter, thinking about the fact that just yesterday the idea of eating here had disgusted her. She made a mental note not to judge people in a place like this and headed for her seat in Josie Pallouchi's theatre. Maybe, there would be meaning behind the mistakes Josie was re-living in her death. Maybe, it would explain some of what she had seen in her father's reel.

Sitting in a red tweed seat, surrounded by that familiar smell of stale popcorn, she closed her eyes falling back into the memory of yesterday. She pictured her father's hand opening the door to the unknown.

*Through the door lie ceilings that would make a bird jealous, with ornate crystal chandeliers. A waltz could be heard playing from some corner of the room while unlikely couples of enormous pink elephants were dancing. They were all painted to look like circus clowns! Dwarfed by their gargantuan waltz, he scrambled to get out from under their feet. This could not be his afterlife, he thought, this was a nightmare. One he knew very well. He spotted the narrator on the other side of the ballroom and started to make his way across.*

*"This?" He exclaimed, pointing to the waltzing couples, "Is my afterlife? This was my daughter's nightmare! My sweet Adrien always felt so small and scared of the things that were out of her control. I spent many nights awake with her helping her get past this dream. But this isn't my dream, what relevance does it have to my death?" The narrator appeared to be in deep thought for a moment, looking out over the crowd of dancers.*

*"Do you still feel like you know everything there is to know about death? Standing among the dancers, do you not feel small? At any moment their feet might crush you, ending all that you thought you knew! Is this not exactly what life felt like before this moment? The uncertainty of it all, the fear of the new and exotic, seeking comfort in the familiar, the safety in the corners of the room, no longer in danger of being seen, or in this case, smashed?" He looked amused by Ben's reaction to the scene.*

As the theatre lights dimmed and the now familiar "Ladies and Gentlemen" announcement played across the house sound system, the memory of yesterday faded away.

"Welcome to the Death-reel of Josie Pallouchi. At 27 years old she was far too young to meet the end. But as we all know, death waits for no man... or woman. She leaves behind two adult cats and her sweet old dog Bruno-Barks. Her next of kin is currently fostering her animals; unfortunately, they cannot keep them due to allergies. If anyone is looking for a companion, you can contact this number after the showing..." The announcer's voice faded away as the screen lit up.

On-screen a young woman was walking into an empty showing house carrying a large bucket of popcorn, a smile on her face, looking cozy in her red sweater and stretchy jeans. She took her seat, her sweater blending into the house chair so well that her body seemed to disappear, leaving behind a floating head waiting for the show to begin. "Ladies and Gentlemen, welcome to the death-reel of Josie Pallouchi..." All joy disappeared from her face as she looked around the empty theatre as if looking for someone to explain to her what she had just heard! It appeared that she hadn't yet realized she had died. Giving up on the absent audience, she turned to face the screen; she stared in disbelief as she saw her image appear.

Josie's reel was what the theatres would call standard nightmare format; she comes to the show expecting to be entertained, but instead, she finds a compilation of every mistake she had ever made. She was watching pivotal moments in her life, moments that altered her way of thinking and changed her path. The audience was captivated by the girl sitting in her empty theatre, all eyes were flitting from her to the memories she was intensely watching. No one wanted to miss her reactions to the hell she was creating on screen.

"Be aggressive! Be! Be! Aggressive!" Pom-poms were flying left, right, and center, the team was practicing on the track beside the football team. Josie was young with a smile that stretched from ear to ear. She led the team in cheer after cheer, sweat coating their uniforms under the late fall sun. During a water break, a player ran up in jersey #1. He was flirting with Josie, and the whole team oohhh'd, and laughed, her face was beet red as she looked down at the turf. The boy smiled and ran back to the field for practice.

After practice, the boy offered to help Josie carry the sound system back to the storage locker. She showed him where to put the system, a familiar rush of heat darkening her cheeks every time he looked at her. When all the equipment had been put away, as she turned to leave, he grabbed her hand. She smiled sweetly looking down at the ground. He pulled her close to him putting his arm around her back. He leaned down to her face and whispered, "Kiss me". She giggled and turned her face into his, his lips enveloping hers. She was smiling again from ear to ear, until he started to move his free hand under her skirt. She reached for his hand to stop it, pulling her face away from his, her smile gone. "I'm not ready for that," she said softly. She didn't want him to leave, but she also didn't want him to go any farther. "Ok," he said, moving his hand up to her face and kissing her again. She relaxed into his kiss. Removing his hand from the small of her back, he used his fingertips to trace the line of her arms, grasping both her hands in his. He slowly raised her hands above her head. Once her hands were together, he gripped both her wrists with one hand. She tried to back away from him, but he'd pushed her up against a wall. He moved his hand back under her skirt. She struggled trying to get her hands free, but it was no use. She tried to scream, but his mouth was covering hers, pressing her head uncomfortably into the wall. He dropped her panties to the floor with his free hand and used his knees to drive her legs apart. He unbuttoned, dropped his pants, and leaned into her. She screamed into his mouth, tears streaking down her face. Her body had stopped responding, he now had control. She was frozen. She couldn't speak. She couldn't move. She closed her still flowing eyes and waited for the assault to stop, he left her body crumpled on the floor of the storage closet, making sure to close the door on his way out.

She lay there until she felt like she could move again. She picked up her ripped panties and sat crying, wondering what to do now. Should she tell someone? No one would believe her; he was so popular, and everyone had seen her flirting with him earlier that day. They would think that she had asked for this. She couldn't tell anyone; that would ruin her life. She got up off the floor and looked for a towel to clean up the blood that was dripping down her legs. She walked home alone. She cried herself to sleep. She went on with her life as if nothing had happened.

The reel cut forward 3 months:

She was stopped on the sidewalk by a group holding up signs. They were screaming about something that she didn't care to hear about. As she pushed through to get where she needed to go, a woman spit in her direction and told her she was going to hell. In the clinic, she sat in the waiting room watching children play, their mothers looking on solemn but determined. She held her hands around the small of her abdomen and wondered what life would be like in the future. Would she be ok? Should she be here? What choice did she have? She couldn't keep this baby. She hadn't wanted a baby. She hadn't wanted to have sex. She wasn't ready. Yet here she was, having to make one of the hardest decisions of her life, one that would stay with her forever. "Josie," the nurse called and led her through a door. When she left the clinic, she was crying holding that small patch of abdomen.

Pain was visible on her face, a pain that never really went away. It was still found in the lines of the eyes of the older woman sitting in her own death-reel, reliving the most painful moment of her life. Adrien didn't have to wonder what emotions Josie was experiencing. She could hear a sigh, soft and gentle, and see Josies shoulders move gently as she cried. There wasn't a dry eye in the theatre.

The big moments being relived shifted to better memories as she aged on screen. Going to college. Getting a job in marketing, not knowing how to refill the ink and toner in the fax machine and accidentally breaking it the first day - the rest of her time there that fax machine only printed documents in Blue or Purple. Rescuing her dog, although she would always say that Bruno rescued her. Picking up her cats from the shelter, a bonded pair who needed to find a home together. On their first night home, they were too scared to come out of the cardboard kennels, so Josie cut one side out of each and pushed the kennels together so they could still be together until they were ready to explore their new home. When they got older, feeling at home, attacking her toes while she slept and scratching up the furniture. They were little tornadoes of claws and chaos and the girl sitting in her own hell looked to be crying, then laughing; what a strange sound to hear in a death-reel. She was taking in these moments one last time. The last thing she watched was her death. She was in a car accident. The figure on screen flinched when the impact rocked the theatre, then watched as first responders arrived on the scene solemn in their work to free her from the vehicle. Josie looked away from her screen towards the exit. It had a faint glow to it, almost too faint to see. She got up, moving towards it. As she reached the door, she took one more look at the mangled wreck and wrapped her hand around the doorknob. She stepped through, then reached behind her, leaning back into the room, looked in the direction of the crowd, and winked - pulling the door shut.

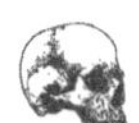

There it was! Had anyone else seen that? A sign that there was something else after the death-reel. Adrian was hooked, deciding to see the rest of the showings featured in Hell today. She stopped back by the snack counter and grabbed a hot dog and a soda before heading into the next viewing house.

Stephanie Madrigal's showing was terrifying, yet comical.

She had drowned on the coast while surfing, a rip current had washed her out too far to swim back to shore. The last thing she saw while floating to the bottom of the ocean was lobsters. This was horrific to watch, but when her hell started it got worse. She was swimming in the sea in no apparent distress. Before long, she felt a stir below the surface. Diving down she discovered the waters full of lobsters with gigantic claws, and she wasn't wearing any footwear. She thrashed about, this way and that, trying to outswim the lobsters. She lost every toe before it ended, the water was no longer clear, it now had a pink hue. She gave up thrashing about when she had nothing left to lose. There wasn't any reprieve from her hell, no doorway to a better place, no hidden meaning behind her reel.

Adrien headed home lost in her thoughts. She must have imagined the wink at the end of the first showing or given it false meaning when it was just a trick of the mind. After all, no one else had noticed anything strange or unusual. There was nothing after the death-reel, a bright empty room of nothing, just like the beginning of her father's showing. She chalked it up to grieving and decided to call it a day. *Besides,* she thought, *nothing good could come from brimstone and fire or watching a man lose his family.*

# CHAPTER THREE

*In the Ballroom, beneath the crystal chandeliers, Ben sat in the opening of a large slide. It had appeared at the far end of the Elephant waltz, above the slide was a label that read Unknown, not looking back he pushed himself forward into what felt like a perpetual fall.*

Startled awake, Adrien looked at the clock, 4 am… She had felt like she was with him, sliding down that slide. Where would it lead her? She wiped the sleep from her eyes and sat up, too awake to fall back asleep, too asleep to leave her bed. She closed her eyes, leaning back against her headboard, and followed her father down the slide.

*After what felt like an eternity, which had been sped up in the theatre, he landed with a smile into a golden ball pit. Looking around he found himself in a strange version of what must have been Heaven. There were so many people, some that he knew who had passed, and some he didn't. The streets were golden, and the scenery was made of dense clouds. The narrator was there waiting for him, he splashed around the ball pit for a minute thinking himself a genius for coming up with something so joyous in his* last moments. Then he followed the narrator down a golden road. Everyone was content, playing together like they hadn't a care; animals were running free and children playing safely. This was a beautiful contrast to anything earthly, yet it seemed familiar like he had seen it all before.

"Do you know where we are?" The narrator asked, "This is where you took everything you learned from teaching the Catholic and Christian religions and married them to create your own Heaven." Ben surveyed his own Heaven, everything, and everyone he ever loved was here! He couldn't help but smile as he watched his sweet Adrien – only a toddler here – playing with Maxwell his favorite puppy. His smile grew as he heard the laughter from his older two children, giggling together over their tea party on a table made of clouds. His wife had never looked more beautiful as she entertained their parents, waving to him and asking him to come sit down and have a glass of sweet tea with them. His smile started to dim.

"None of this is real?" Ben asked half-heartedly, not wanting to know the answer.

The Narrator replied, "Although your family hasn't passed, and you have known many versions of them throughout your life, these are the ones you imagined here." Ben was silent, realizing that this was just another dream, this time, not really heaven, or hell; Not real. They continued down the road, at the end, he turned back to look at all the happy faces one last time. A tear slipped down his cheek, knowing he had no choice but to leave them behind. He turned again and found another slide labeled Unknown. He took his place and pushed forward.

Adrien opened her eyes to a beeping sound coming from the kitchen, coffee was ready, 6 am. She got up and contemplated her father's time in heaven. Heaven was such a strange concept, you create a world full of the people you've loved and lost, a place outside of time, emotion, and everything that makes a human human. You go there to wait for your family to join you. Then, they get there years later, and they keep you company while they wait for their loved ones to join them, and so on. It must be crowded there, the only place you can go to wait for your loved ones to die. Maybe this wasn't what heaven was for everyone. How could she really know if she didn't go find out for herself?

Adrien headed back to the theatres, this time in search of Heaven. She needed to know what heaven meant to those who imagined that fate. *Heaven* (the theatre) looked much more peaceful than *Hell*. Walking up to the theatre the first things to catch Adrien's eye were the perfectly manicured lawns, lined with white rock flower beds, and complete with topiaries in the shape of animals. The outside of the building was warm and inviting, made entirely of white marble, the front windows were embellished with colored glass giving the illusion they were inset with jewels. The interior walls were covered floor to ceiling with bright blue skies full of clouds; their decorators were genius; no expense was spared in selling their brand.

The showings in this theatre were a little different, they had a section of classics including Benjamin Franklin and Napoleon Bonaparte; historical figures that had been embalmed when buried were often able to have reels extracted.

However, the quality of a reel extracted from a poorly preserved corpse is low-grade. The better the preservation of the body, the better the quality of the reel. Then they had current deaths with obituary descriptions.

The oldest reel available belonged to a man whose body was preserved in a peat bog. It was titled 'Tollund Man - Human Sacrifice' and it is believed that he lived between 405 & 384 BCE. Today's newcomers were Mindy Applebaum - who died in a bathtub, Frank Taub - who died peacefully in his sleep, and Martha Mosby - who discovered a seafood allergy a little too late in life.

"Ladies and Gentlemen, Frank Taub was a larger-than-life man. He lived every day to the fullest, always ready for an adventure! He is succeeded by his wife and 4 adult sons. Frank was 67 years old when he passed, still an active member of his community and an all-around good guy! He believed that actions spoke louder than words and lived his life by that conviction. To honor him we will let his reel speak for itself." There was a hint of admiration in the announcer's voice as he trailed off and the showing began.

On-screen, Frank was reliving his last day before falling into eternal sleep. He'd gotten up, stretched, and went out to grab the mail patting his golden retriever on the head as he passed. "Good morning, Alice," he said cheerfully. He took the mail and his daily newspaper to the table to read to his wife while she made their morning coffee. He placed them down on the table and walking up behind her he wrapped his arms around her waist; a smile spread between them. They held each other like this for a moment, he kissed her shoulder and then returned to the paper.

"Honey! Did you see this? The mayor approved the city's plan to make crosswalks for squirrels! Apparently, the little buggers have been running out into traffic and the city has wanted to do something to save them. Well, it took him long enough to approve this!" A smirk lit up his face as he looked expectantly at his wife.

"Did he really?" She asked curiously, not looking up from her chore... His silence answered her question, as she glanced up from the freshly filled coffee cups and saw him snickering at her. "Oh! You!" was all she could get out before she started laughing with him. "Squirrel crosswalks, I don't know how I could've fallen for that one!" She joined him at the table, handing him a cup and he held her hand up to his mouth, gently kissing it. Playful banter accompanied their morning of news and coffee, the love they felt for each other shone through the screen and had the entire audience swooning. After breakfast, he kissed his wife and headed out for his morning walk.

Equipped with a small bag and a grabbing stick, he picks up garbage around his neighborhood. Waving to each of his neighbors as he passes by, some stop him to ask for advice, some smile and thank him for his diligence, everyone waves back. When he returns home, he gets ready to head out to work. Lucky enough to be retired, he still volunteers his time at a meals-on-wheels kitchen making sure that the elderly who are less active in his community are being taken care of. He gets home around 5 p.m. for dinner with his wife, they do the dishes together talking about their days, and end the night dancing together in the kitchen. Then they head up to bed, where he falls asleep - unknowingly - for the last time.

A man enters the room and reaches out for Frank's spirit. Free from his body he looks lovingly at his wife one last time, at peace with the life he is now leaving behind. He turns to the man and says, "Show me the way" he follows the man to a grand staircase. When he reached the top of the staircase he crossed a pearl gate, entering an oasis of palm trees, squinting against the blinding light. There are many roads all leading nowhere, as there was nowhere left to go, and mansions as far as the eye could see. When his eyes had adjusted to the heavenly light he said, "I am Home." No longer plagued by his earthly body he ran, played with the animals, and met family and friends who had been waiting for him. He didn't stop to think of the family he had left behind, secure in the knowledge that one day they would join him here.

Frank's imagination was a biblically accurate description of heaven. His death-reel was short and sweet. Frank's life and death had taken up an hour of screen time, but his afterlife was exiguous moments; not even thirty minutes into his Heaven it ended. He was happily living his ever after, with no need for more. Fading to nothing was not even noticed in the end, he was completely consumed by the perfect world that his mind had created as the film reel started to fade away until the screen was black. All traces of Frank Taub were left in his reel and in the hearts of the loved ones he had left behind.

Adrien had many more questions when she left the viewing house. She thought about the short reel, were some people okay with death? Was she okay with death? Are beliefs strong enough to fight fear? What did she believe in? Was information causing more unease about the afterlife? That couldn't be true, her father had taught her not to fear the unknown her entire life. If ignorance really was bliss, then why did people come to the theatres? Why was she still coming to the theatres? Filled with curiosity she headed into the Tollund Man's death-reel. If his reel was the oldest available for viewing, maybe, he could answer her newest questions.

"Ladies and Gentlemen, this is a special opportunity to see the reel of a man from the Iron Age! The Tollund Man was discovered in a Peat Bog in Denmark. Not much was known about his mummified body until Death-reel tech unlocked the secrets hidden inside his mind! Bear witness to the life - and death - of a true Viking."

As the reel began to spin there was a low gurgling noise that accompanied the opalescent picture. It appears that the bog has seeped into the reel staining the film and creating an underwater effect for the viewers. The gurgling sound system erupted filling the house with a cacophony of screams. Immediately the showing house filled with an uproar of men. The hazy screen showed a field of men preparing for battle, young and old alike! The crowd parted as a berserker walked among the men, those surrounding him would quiet and look in his direction showing respect with a nod. There was no doubt this man would lead them into battle. With a wave of his hand, a hush spread over the crowd.

"Rrraaaaaahhhhhhh!" Screamed the Berserker and the men went wild! The screams were earsplitting, blood-curdling, primal, guttural. He allowed them to get their energy out for a moment before asking for silence again with another wave of his hand.

"Brethren, I have come to you with a plea! The Gods require one among us to come forward and take his place by the side of Odin. One who will face death with pride and wake to find himself in Valhalla among the best of us! Will you be our sacrifice?" The crowd was silent as they looked at one another, who would be brave enough to sacrifice himself for the good of all? Who would take their leader to be with Odin for strength and strategy in battle?

Then one man called out, "Aye, I will give my life for those of my brothers! I will die so that others may live! Give me this honor of being with Odin, and I shall bring you luck in the coming war." Although he looked feeble, he was prepared to die a warrior's death. His actions showed that he was as much a warrior as every other man on the battlefield that day. The men cheered, lifting him onto their shoulders, this night he would feast like a king on fish and porridge, tomorrow he would fast to cleanse his body for the sacrifice! The cheers of the men surrounding him began to fade away as the gurgling took over the sound system again. The reel's picture didn't fade so much as submerge in a thick slimy substance bubbling as it sank. Remnants of the turbid water from the bog which had left its mark on the record of this Vikings life.

The next memory to play was him being washed and dressed. His attendants lifted him upon a horse and led him to a sacrificial tree. He sat tall upon the horse as a noose was tied around his neck, thrown over a branch. Cheering erupted through the crowd as several men hoisted him into the air. Struggling with every breath, eyes bloodshot and bulging, he watched the leader sit below him, praying to the Gods for favor from this sacrifice. He watched until a dark fog started to creep into his vision, the Berserker below him forever seared into his mind. The sound of the men cheering faded as the soft gurgling noises of the reel persisted and bubbles floated across the screen as murky water enveloped the film, everything faded to black, and the scene cut out.

As the viewing house illuminated the big screen was showing the man standing in a field. He blinked incredulously as his hands roamed over his face and body, where he had once been old and feeble, his body was restored to its former glory. His hands stopped at the rope around his neck, cautiously he removed it letting it fall to the ground. Satisfied with his new condition he surveyed the field, not too far in the distance stood a grand hall. The Hall was golden, gleaming in the light, a stark contrast to its surroundings. As he neared the entrance, he found himself surrounded by wolves, a low snarl reverberated through their chest as they bared their teeth in his direction. He glanced up at the sky noticing eagles flying above, circling him as if he were their next meal. He took a step forward with a knowing smile, placed his hands firmly against the doors, pushed them open, and stepped into the hall. The roof was made of shields, and the rafters made of spears, and the grand tables before him were overflowing with a magnificent feast! He took his seat at the table and was welcomed with a cheer!

The rest of the reel was severely damaged, with clips of battles fought and friendships forged! A clip of the army following a large white-haired man adorned with a helmet laden with antlers, a fur cape draped over his shoulders, and riding atop an eight-legged horse. He held a spear in one hand and blew a horn signaling the start of a battle. Tollund man rode into every battle face hardened, showing no sign of fear. Another clip depicted the warrior in the grand hall being served by Valkyrie and failing miserably to flirt with them. The crowd in the theatre laughed, Tollund Man was where he felt he belonged, in the last clip he was riding into battle towards a great light, and without a glance back he rode his horse into the light at full gallop, spear at the ready. The reel ended with the gurgling noise dominating the sound system as the film appeared to sink back into the bog and cut to black.

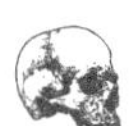

How can everyone have such differing perceptions of Heaven?

Why did some people make a door to exit their reels at the end and others didn't? Was there more beyond the reel or was this a common belief held by those who created the door for themselves? She had naively believed that going to the theatres was supposed to answer all her questions about death; it was supposed to ruin her afterlife by showing her all the answers, but the death-reels always left her with more questions.

# CHAPTER FOUR

After dinner, Adrien picked up the phone to call her mother. She played with the rotary, absentmindedly dialing each number. She had never owned a cellphone; she liked the whimsy that having an older phone with an answering machine added to her life. As she watched the dial spin on the last number, she thought about her father's reel.

*riiing*

*Benjamin lay back into the slide, it was a long way down, it felt like an eternity to reach the bottom. The slide abruptly ended with his ass skidding across a hot floor. By the time he got to his feet, his pants were smoldering. It took him a moment to realize where he was. "Hell... I'm in Hell now? I didn't think this would make an appearance in my afterlife..." Ben's voice exclaimed, shocked, and amused by his surroundings.*

*"You thought you were making up your own story?" Asked the Narrator.*

*"That's what everyone thinks! We make it up, this is my imagination and to be honest it has not yet disappointed me. Although Hell seems a little unoriginal, my bottom has already*

*interacted with its unpleasantness."* Ben laughed at his own joke, and the narrator looked on disapprovingly.

**riiing**

*"Let's go see what your version of Hell includes, shall we."* With that, the narrator stepped aside allowing Ben to take the lead in this new terrain.

*Fire and Brimstone; the whole place was a dimly lit corridor of black rock with lava streams and cracks in the rock faces. The glow of the lava cast an orange-red hue on the world around them. With such poor lighting and the trick of the fire and shadow, visibility was nil. Ben almost missed the first door on his right, it was not labeled unknown, it was labeled Adrian.*

*"No." it was the only word he could choke out, the door opened to reveal his daughter burning in eternal flame. His nostrils were flooded with the smell of burning flesh. Her screams were deafening as she cried out for him to save her. Ben barreled into the room trying to scoop her up in his arms and take her pain away, but his arms moved right through her. The flames licked at his skin with nothing more than the sensation of a tickle while they ripped screams that turned his insides to puddles from his daughter's mouth. The heat was so intense that his tears evaporated from his eyes before they could touch his face, jaw clenched, he turned... and walked away. "It's made up, she's safe." He muttered to himself over and over again as he came to another door, this one labeled Sarah, his wife. He refused to look in at the image, he could hear her screams, pleading with him to come save her. He couldn't bear to see the hell he had condemned her to. He continued, each step harder than the last. "It's all in my head, they're safe, it's all in my head," he continually told himself as more doors appeared along the*

*abhorred hallway.*

*riiing*

A tear slipped down Adrien's cheek.

*He kept his eyes straight ahead, determined to escape, almost missing the door labeled Unknown. His entire body was steaming from the sweat that didn't stay, it evaporated as soon as he produced it. His hand reached for the handle; he cried out in pain as it seared into his skin but refused to stay in this personal Hell even a second longer. He pulled the door open and stepped inside without ever looking back.*

***

"Hello?" her mother answered.

"H-hi Mom, it's me," she replied pulling herself from the memory and wiping the tears from her face. "I wanted to check on you, we haven't gotten the chance to talk since… Dad's reel."

"Hi honey, it's nice to hear your voice. I haven't felt much like visiting with anyone quite yet. I sure do miss your father." A quiet sob came through the line, and she tried to stifle it, "I love you, how are you little honeybee?"

"Oh, mom! I'm so sorry I haven't been over! I've been processing in my own way… I've been, going to the theatres, to try to make sense of Dad's reel. I just don't…"

"Going to the theatres!?" Her mother cut her off, "Why? Your father always told you not to go! Imagine him gone for less than a week and you're already forgetting his wishes!" Adrien could hear the hurt in her voice accompanied by the tears her mother was no longer fighting.

"I know! Mom, I know! I just don't understand! Why was his reel like that? What did it mean? Is it really all in..."

"It doesn't matter, he wouldn't want us to turn our backs on everything that he stood for in life!"

"Mom, you saw the same reel that I did! You were there in that theatre! Aren't you the least bit curious?" Adrien could hear the desperation in her own voice. She wanted to know what it all meant so badly, bad enough to go against her father's wishes and search for her own answers. She wanted her mother to understand. Adrien knew that their grief wasn't the same, she knew her mother couldn't understand, or wouldn't. "Let's just... spend some time together, okay? Can we just, be on the phone? - I need you."

"I would love that. I'll stay on the phone as long as you need. I need you too, we all grieve in our own way."

They stayed like that for hours, both just holding their phones and listening to the presence on the other line; no longer alone. Adrien didn't hang up until she heard her mother's breathing even out and knew that the worst of the crying was over, she needed rest and it would be selfish to keep it from her. They could process together later, when it didn't hurt so badly, when it wasn't as fresh. She made a mental note to take her mother a casserole later that day and make sure she was eating, then she got ready and headed to *Hell*.

Today's showings were a worldwide sensation Albert Rogers - died in bed, Melinda Missey - cardiac arrest, and a few familiar names, her fathers included. She cringed when she saw Stephanie Madrigal's name still on the marquee, who knew bloodthirsty lobsters would be such a hit? She wasn't ready to view her father's reel again, surprised it was still available to the public given its length and she tucked into Albert Rogers theatre.

"Ladies and Gentlemen... Albert Rogers leaves behind nothing, not a penny to his name, as you will see the stripper took care of that, and no one to call his own." The announcer's voice died away as the lights dimmed and Albert Rogers took the screen naked as the day he was born. He jumped into bed with some woman- presumably the stripper - and began making passionate love in every imaginable position. He was quite athletic for being a stoutly man with a comb-over. He settled her on top of him and suddenly his spirit was being pulled through the bed, down at such speed he didn't have time to process, trying to cling to the non-existent walls, flailing about, anything to slow the fall. What a surprise for his unsuspecting lover, the $200 in his wallet isn't enough to pay for the therapy she's going to need after this. Down he was pulled through an ever-present darkness, down against nothingness until his spirit gave in and he stopped fighting the air, resigned to his fate. Down until he landed on the brimstone floor of his own personal Hell.

"Well, I guess I deserve this," was the only thing he said as he looked down and realized that his afterlife would be on broadcast in his birthday suit. He was in a circular room, hot enough that he was already dripping sweat despite having just arrived. He chose a door and walked through, on the other side was a beautiful woman, she motioned for him to come in, the door closed behind him. He walked up to her and was met with a deep kiss, he started to strip away her clothes as she kissed his face, and while each article of clothing was removed, he heard her moan and leaned deeper into the kiss. When he was satisfied with his work, he pulled back to admire her body only to reveal that she was *still fully clothed*. Disappointed he started to undress her again, his anticipation grew with each layer he removed, yet as he removed the last article of clothing she was suddenly fully dressed again. No matter how he tried he couldn't seem to keep her clothes off, all the while her moaning growing louder; he couldn't look away from the pleading in her eyes for him to relieve her of this desire. The audience laughed harder with his every try; his personal hell had become a worldwide comedy.

After realizing that no matter what he tried he would never be able to disrobe this moaning woman he ran for the door, back to the brimstone and fire. In the hall, he counted seven doors and wondered if each one would be equally frustrating. He opened the next door, "can't be worse than that, can it?"

Inside he found a tv playing in the center of the room, every channel was porn. Looking around the room he was surrounded by bookshelves loaded with dirty magazines. He saw a cozy chair and a stand with lotion and napkins, sat down, and began to watch the TV. As the scene before his eyes grew more animated, his face showed his excitement; he grabbed the napkins in anticipation when suddenly his face fell, he was holding his limp dick in his hands. He looked at it with frustration, where was his climax? He put the napkins back and continued to watch the program, he went back to work to relieve himself, and again as he reached his peak, he went limp with no success. He changed channels. He looked through magazines instead of watching TV. He changed positions. He was desperate for a release, but it never came. By the time he left this room, he was raw, and his spirit was broken.

Back in the circular room he went, unable to sit as the floor was too hot for his bare ass. Should he try another door? There must be something better than this, he might at least be able to relieve himself if he were in a different room. He opened a third door and stepped inside.

Inside this room was a strip club, his smile spread from ear to ear as the announcer in the club said, blowjobs are free today only! He found a seat at the end of the catwalk and spread his bare legs wide to show the girls what he was working with. He watched a beautiful redhead saunter down the runway to a pole at the end, she was dressed in leather from head to toe. She purred at him as she grabbed the pole and started to dance. His mouth gaped open at the ends as if he were in a trance. When she finished her dance, she came off the stage and bent forward, her cleavage hanging inches from his nose.

"Would you like me to take some of these clothes off?" She whispered to him.

"Yes, please Baby!" He exclaimed. His eyes were glued to her every movement as she reached her arms behind her to release her zipper. She pulled it free and started to take her leather suit off, leaving behind red where black had once been, he looked startled. As he leaned in to see what was under her suit, she pulled it free with a sigh of relief, dropping it on the floor. He realized that her skin was stuck to the suit! As she removed her mask, the skin on her face peeled with it. He tried to get up and leave, but her bare muscled body was straddling him, skin drooping where it was still attached.

"Don't you want me baby?" She exclaimed as she kissed his mouth. He shook his head violently, trying to push her mutilated body off him. She glanced around the room for the other girls to come help. They came over and held him down in his chair while the redhead wrapped her mouth around him. On either side of him were women who looked more dead than alive, one was missing an eye and maggots were falling out of her empty socket, the other was all skin and bone, she didn't look to have a muscle or an organ in her body. He screamed as he was held in place, he screamed when his orgasm started to spill out of the redhead's mouth and all over his lap.

"Yummy!" She giggled, tears streaming down his face. "Who's next?" They all took turns pleasuring him while the others held him down in the chair. When they were done, they let him up and he ran from the room. "Come see us again!" They called after him.

He ran from room to room, opening doors, looking for a way out, a place to hide, but the horrors in the other rooms were worse than what he had already suffered. Exhausted, he closed all the doors around him, his frantic search had been fruitless, and he gave up. His body slunk to the floor in the middle of the round room, his bare ass sizzling on the brimstone, the smoke from his burning pubic hair wafting up to his nose. He sobbed as the theatre faded to black.

*What in the hell did I just watch?* Adrien thought to herself as she left the theatre. *What kind of life did a man have to live to condemn himself to such a disgusting Hell? Worldwide sensation... the world is full of sick freaks who like to watch other people's torment.* Then again, she had sat through the entire showing, maybe she was just another one of those sick freaks? She decided that Hell can be whatever you make it.

# CHAPTER FIVE

Adrien lay in bed watching the glow of traffic lights dance across the plastic stars on her ceiling. The gap above her curtains let in a little too much light on nights like this. As the traffic slowed and the lights went from near constant to scarce, her body relaxed into an uncomfortable sleep.

A blue man was chasing her, wielding swords in his many arms. She ran this way and that, ducking blows and running through massive thorny plants she'd never seen before. She tripped on upturned roots and rolled until her body hit something. She lay still under a giant mushroom bloom, watching large blue feet walk by, *why was he chasing her?* Suddenly, the mushroom was unearthed, he knelt above her swords at the ready, *those eyes, they looked... so familiar, where had she seen those eyes?* His swords came down, she awoke in bed gasping for breath, the dream so vivid was already fading away, all except those eyes. Eyes that had known the universe and all its wonder. Eyes that, if given the chance to lose oneself in them, could teach you the secrets of the world.

4 am. This was becoming a habit, instead of trying to sleep

she got up and made her coffee early, a little stronger to help make it through the day. She was going to head back to the theatre today, not meaning to make this a habit, but curious about what others believed. Maybe the man in her dreams made an appearance in others' dreams; Afterall, hadn't she first seen him in her father's reel?

On her walk to the theatre, she recalled her father's reel, where she had first seen those eyes. He had just left Hell through the Unknown door without looking back.

*Benjamin walked through a room filled with podiums, he looked around wondering if he had somehow made it into an alternative Hell where Congress would be his judge and jury. Chuckling to himself he walked to the center of the room. Looking out over the crowd of empty podiums he saw figures start to appear. 'Full house' he thought as he looked on trying to recognize faces and figures. In attendance was the one God in his three forms, Zeus, Hera, and all of the Olympians, Brahma, Vishnu in his many avatars, Shiva, his wife Parvati and son Ganesha, Odin, Hel, Thor, Loki, the Egyptian gods; Re, Osiris, Anubis, and more filled the room. Spinning on his heels he saw gods take their places at the podiums and thought to himself, this is something only my brain would make up.*

*All of these deities had been a part of his job, being a death curator Ben had worked with thousands of people building their belief systems around these religious figures. He was familiar with each one; Ganesha was the elephant-headed Hindu god, he is the remover of obstacles, and Re is the Egyptian god of the sun. It amused him that they had all shown up in his afterlife, how fitting that figures that he had contemplated in life, would now give him an audience in death.*

*"Benjamin Burnum," There he was, the blue man with the many sword-wielding arms. "You have been brought before us as a disciple of all. We are not here to ask you to choose, we have decided you belong with all of us. You have led many to faith and affirmed their beliefs throughout your life. We grant you council in this time of transition." The film cuts out at this moment, there were some technical difficulties with the reel. A brief intermission was had while the film was repaired. When it cut back in Ben had a look of contentment on his face and he was heading to the back of the room, to the one empty podium, labeled Unknown.*

What had he talked to the gods about? Whatever the conversation held, it seemed to satisfy him. Adrien wished she could've been there, more to hear her father's questions than to hear the answers provided. Although, she assumed they both came from his mind, so they were probably both equally interesting.

She reached *Heaven* and read today's Obit Posters, most of the reels available last time she visited, were still playing. *Hell* seemed to cycle through reels, but heavens were so pleasant that they stuck around. The newer screenings were Gerald McMinagain - Aneurism in the Bathroom, Deval Sandri - Heist Gone Wrong, and Phillis Nidus - Heart Attack at Work.

"Ladies and Gentlemen... Deval Sandri was a world-renowned thief; he was so good at what he did that he was called the ghost, no one saw him come or the art he was stealing leave.  He is survived by two loving parents, eight siblings, and many many nieces and nephews. He leaves behind his hedgehog named Cactus, and an extensive art collection that has been seized by governing officials."

Adrien picked this one because she was curious how a thief ended up in heaven, maybe he had stolen his afterlife as well. The lights dimmed and the reel began to play.

Flashbacks of all his escapades played on screen, his life had been full of mischief, all followed by his most recent endeavor. He was belaying through the glass roof of a museum looking to steal a new Art exhibit for his collection, when the rope slipped on the ledge breaking a panel in the roof and sending glass falling towards him. Even though he tried to swing out of the way it was too late, he was skewered with a piece of glass and bled to death hanging from the ceiling. His spirit climbed the rope to the roof where he met Shiva. He was to face reincarnation not knowing who he would become, but he was sure he had done enough wrong in this life, that he would spend many lifetimes making up for it.

The screen faded and returned on a grassy plane, he was a grasshopper, his thoughts played aloud even though he couldn't speak. He had a memory of his previous life and knew this was his first chance at redemption. As a grasshopper he didn't need much, just a name to call himself. He could no longer be Deval Sandri, he would now be Ishanyu, Full of Strength, and strength he would need to learn to be a grasshopper. His mind was active at first as he learned to navigate his new life, but as he sought companionship, his muted disposition allowed his thoughts to recede into silence. He learned to chirp with his legs and make music for the villagers working in nearby fields. He found a mate and started populating his home. He had thousands of children, all of whom he taught to hop and chirp and live alongside their human and animal companions. Then there came a drought, a famine for the humans of the land. Ishanyu led by example, knowing their fate, he sought out the humans and sacrificed himself for their sustenance, his children, and their children for generations (generations being so short for a grasshopper) sacrificed their lives to feed the people of the land, knowing that when the people were taken care of, they would replenish the land and their descendants would live on forever. His spirit was released from his grasshopper body and was met by Brahma. Brahma explained that because of his sacrifice and his devotion to the people of the land, he would be reborn again as a child, he would lose the memories of his past lives as he grew but could regain them in this life if he wished through meditation. He was warned that focusing on the past can be as hurtful as it can be rewarding. His name would henceforth be Nimit, which meant destiny, and this life would be his opportunity to create a new destiny for himself.

He grew up alongside the grasshoppers that he had sired, he played with them and listened to their songs, always feeling a strange comfort from their presence. He no longer had memories of Deval or Ishanyu, they faded out as he had grown. He was now Nimit, a poor boy, he worked alongside his mother and brothers tending the land, restoring life where there was once only drought.

At four years old he was an inquisitive boy, asking questions the entire day. On his way to fetch water, while walking in the fields, sowing seeds, pulling weeds and planting trees. He asked of everything; What is the sky? Why do the birds fly? Why do we plant the seeds? How did the world work before me? Will I live forever? Why do the grasshoppers sing? --- His mother answered all his questions as she knew, never losing patience with her little one. The sky is a sea of stars, it is where the Gods go to play, and it was given to us so that we would always see the beauty and vastness of the world. The birds fly because that is how the Gods made them, they were made to soar above the ground collecting seeds and spreading them throughout the world so we may eat new things as they travel. We sow seeds so we may eat, for a long time all we had to eat were the grasshoppers, they would come to us, a gift from the earth, and we would eat what we needed to survive until we could restore the land for them to live. We sow the seeds to give back for their sacrifice and to restore the earth for she wishes to grow and feed her children. The grasshoppers sing because they are happy, we are giving back to them and they are rejoicing, their song is thanks for their future, and we listen to remind us that all is connected. Yes, son, we will live forever. As long as we are good and follow the Trimurti, we will live many lives, this is but one. We are meant to restore the earth, to serve our brothers and sisters, and to walk with grace and virtue. These answers didn't stop his questioning, he continued throughout the years.

At the age of sixteen, he was sent by his mother to study the scriptures and practices that could make him a leader among their village. He was gone for a year and returned to continue his life of study at the village temple. Under the guidance of the Pandit, he learned to perform puja and lead the people of their village in worship.

At the age of thirty, he succeeded his Pandit and became the leader of the temple. He led the village in worship to the Trimurti and he forged public relations between his village and the neighboring villages. He would draw attention to his teachings with stories of his lives, remembered through meditative practices. His mother was proud to call him her son, and he was proud to be living a life that Brahma and Shiva could be proud of.

At the age of eighty, he trained his successor in the temple, and he worked with leaders of the nation to heal their connection to the earth. He taught his belief that all were connected and that we will be reborn in lives that will help us understand what we have missed and help us reach nirvana. He still sat outside his house at night and listened to the grasshoppers, recalling everything that his mother had taught him when he was a little boy.

When he was ready to leave his human life he gathered his family, friends, and followers, and he addressed them one last time. He was not to be worshiped as a man, for he was only a man, he was to be remembered as a humble servant of the Gods. A reminder that they are always watching, always among us. They provide what is needed, they allow growth and change, and they are as forgiving as they are vengeful.

He passed in peace and his spirit walked through the praying crowd and met Vishnu at the end of the gathering. Vishnu explained his next lifetime to him, he had done good bringing peace and prosperity to the land and learning from his mistakes. Now it was time for him to find his own inner peace. He would be reborn again, as a tree, and he was to be given the name Manan - thinking to reflect - for in this life he would be an observer, and he could live forever if he had the will to do so.

And so, his life began as Manan, he was a sapling, planted by the followers in the village in their efforts to reforest the land after the drought and famine. He was given memories of his previous lives to reflect upon as he grew. He was surrounded by many other plants and watched as animals passed by or flew overhead. His thoughts about his life were many at first but as the years began to pass and he grew, his memories were etched into the rings of his trunk and his thoughts grew silent of the past and focused on the present. He watched as generations of animals were born and raised, and as the town grew and expanded. He was in awe of the teachings of his previous life still being upheld in the land. As the town expanded, they made sure to keep the balance with nature by not over harvesting, and always giving back as much or more than they took. He watched as first loves snuck into the forest and sought shade below his canopy; he was still as they carved scars into his trunk to mark their love for one another. He grew for over a hundred years, in awe of the world that surrounded him, then his trunk was needed for expansion, so he was chopped down by a woodsman, yet he lived on in his stump, and as the years passed, again he grew from a shoot off the side of his stump back into a leaning tower among the forest trees. He watched as his town failed and the humans left, and the world was quiet and peaceful again. He watched as new people populated the abandoned village, growing it into an empire. He watched season after season, and life after life. He watched leaders rise and fall, all the while the world kept turning, and he kept growing. Throughout the years he had one ever-present companion, Vishnu as many of his avatars would come to visit him, sitting in his shade to meditate and talk of the life he was living. He would recount stories of love and loss and rejoice in the beauty that was the changing leaves of autumn or the falling snow of the winter months. Even after centuries of life, he could still see the beauty in the forest animals whose patterns were reflective of their ancestors' markings, and the euphoria he could still feel every time the wind would greet his canopy, shaking him as no other force on the earth could. He continued like this until he had experienced all that life had to offer him, then he asked Vishnu the last question he ever had. What was the point? If everything that ever was and ever will be, will come to an end, then what was the point in the living, in the breathing, in the everyday? In the mundane life there are such beauties as the fast flapping of a hummingbird's wings, and the slow fall of the first fallen leaf of autumn. It is beautiful, one of a kind even in repetition throughout the years; it will never truly be made the same. Then he answered his own question, everything that ever was, must end to make room for everything that is to be. Without the end, there can be no new beginnings. If life were endless, it wouldn't be special any longer, it would just be. The things that make you excited, the things that light up your soul wouldn't exist after the first hundred years of experiencing them in repetition. Vishnu reached into the tree and pulled Manan's spirit free, "you will come with me," he said, and they walked together through the forest, fading away as the screen faded to black.

Adrien sat in her seat thinking of the blue-faced God who had tried to slay her in her sleep, why had he looked out into the audience as though he knew there were masses watching him? Maybe the man who had passed had seen reels where he was, and this influenced his depiction of his God.

Finally rising to her feet, Adrien felt stiff from sitting through an 8-hour screening. How intricate his lives had been! How he painted his afterlife in such amazing colors! He couldn't have been to a theatre, not with that much belief in his religion. When she exited the theatre, it was nearing 5 o'clock, she would pick up dinner and head to her mother's house to make sure she was eating before heading home for the night. She wondered what her mother thought of reincarnation, her father believed it was a splendid afterlife, one where we punish and reward ourselves. It was truly the best way to feel like we paid our Karma and still got the rewards we so deeply desired of an afterlife.

# CHAPTER SIX

4 am, no surprise. The energy she now had at this hour seemed foreign. She didn't even want to go back to bed. She started the coffee, tidied the kitchen, and took a shower. She was able to read and write in her journal all that she had been thinking about this week's events and the afterlives she hadn't imagined were so intricate and so personal it felt wrong to watch. *The deceased weren't around to care,* she thought, *if they were most of them wouldn't be embarrassed, except naked in Hell guy.*

Dear Diary,                              June 9th, 2062

How is it that I could know my father, spend a lifetime with him by my side, and not have a clue what was going on inside his mind? Being a death curator, I knew he was exposed to all of these religions, I knew that he helped others create their afterlives, but I didn't really know what that meant until this week. "Don't go to the theatre" he used to say, but now it doesn't matter. I wonder what the room of Gods had talked to him about. Too bad the film burnt up at that part, it probably would've been the most interesting to watch! I guess we will never know, all those gods in the same room, and no one looked like they were going to get smited, smite? smote? Then he walked to the Unknown podium and stood behind it, disappearing, moments later reappearing in a courtroom, he was on trial, facing every mistake he had ever made in his life. There were minor offenses like when he was a boy, he stole a piece of candy from the local grocery store. When he was a teenager just old enough to drive, he broke every rule of the road. He was lucky to stay alive long enough to meet my mother. Meeting her had slowed him down, he had something, someone to live for. When the judge started reading the offences he'd committed during their marriage, my family and I couldn't help but laugh! "You took her favorite coffee mug and pretended that you didn't realize, why would you do that?" and Ben answered "I wanted to have a piece of her close to me even after she left for work. And then we cried, he was such a loving man, he had lived a full life, and all his offenses had been minimal, comical. When the judge was satisfied with all his answers, he was allowed to leave judgment. The narrator, who had played the part of the bailiff, led him to a set of doors labeled Unknown. Did he believe in judgment day? It was hard to tell what he believed because there was so much to process. I need to find answers to the questions that I have. I think I will go to Heaven today and find a new afterlife to see) Afterall, it's no longer forbidden to go to the theatres.

Honeybee

She always signed her diary Honeybee; it was her father's nickname for her, and she loved the way it looked sprawled out in cursive hand. She thought about never hearing him say it to her again and tears trickled down her face into her mug of no longer hot coffee.

The new reels showing in Heaven were Zarian Parkinzie - Struck by lightning, and Allison Westbank - Died in the Hospital. Both reels were relatively short at 2 hours each, but Zarian's reel was so unusual that she hoped that such a strange, unexpected death would spark a different death reel. Even if it wasn't, she had enough time to sit through both his and Allison's reels.

"Ladies and Gentlemen... Zarian Parkinzie was a man of few

words; he enjoyed spending his time with his close family and his animals. His most prized possession in the world was his parakeet named Rexy. He believed that birds, being the descendants of dinosaurs, should be named after them. He is survived by his Bird, two cats, and his parents. He will be missed by the town that he served as their mayor before the unexpected incident took his life." The theatre lights faded away and his last day popped up on screen. He was taking a walk on his lunch break; he looked like he was stressed with the day's work but as soon as he stepped outside all the worry melted off his face. He looked up to the sky, the clouds were beautiful, fierce, and threatening at the same time. He expected rain, a storm was imminent, but he needed to clear his head, so he headed out for a short walk hoping to beat the weather. He made it to the end of the parking lot before being struck down by lightning. His spirit steamed out of his body and was immediately whisked away to a new room. (Adrien was thankful that she didn't have to experience the aftermath of that lightning strike) "Hello, Mr. Parkinzie," a man in white robes said.

"Uh, h-hello" was his timid reply.

"Ever the shy man! That's ok, you don't have to talk much, but we do need to discuss... some things." The man wrapped his arm around Zarian's shoulders and started to lead him, "Let's finish that walk, shall we?"

The man walked with Mr. Parkinzie until it seemed that the shock of his sudden demise had worked its way through his system, and he became more responsive. Then, Zarian started to recognize the scenery; they were walking along the drive to his childhood home.

"I know this place." He choked out, a look of surprise on his face. "What are we doing here?"

"This is where your life began, this is where our journey together begins. When you were just a boy your family loved you more than you can imagine, let's look in!" They looked in through the window and all of Zarian's childhood memories played out before him. Losing his tooth and watching his parents sneak quarters under his pillow, opening gifts on Christmas and birthdays, reading books in the rocking chair with his mother's arms around him, learning how to build a fire with his dad, and all the hugs, toys, kisses, goodnights, and good mornings that came with growing up in such a loving family. Tears trickled down his face as he looked in on the memory of his childhood.

"They'll be devastated when they find out that I've passed, but they'll have my reel to know that I didn't suffer and, in the end, I thought of them! I wish I had been a better son and visited more." He allowed the man to lead him away, they continued their walk. Coming upon his high school, they found a window and looked in. He saw before him hallways loaded with children, young Zarian was walking down the hall, and everyone knew him. Even back then he didn't talk much, but he was so kind when he did, that all he ever made were friends. He had won the heart of his high school crush in these hallways, and she had become his wife when they had graduated. He saw himself in clubs, joining activist groups, and writing for the school newspaper. "What a life I've lived. I never had to pretend to be someone I wasn't. People seemed to accept me being quiet and gave me some of my best years here. I was extremely lucky to make the friends I did!"

The man led him away, he came upon a church, decorated inside and out, he looked through the stained-glass windows and saw his wedding day. His bride had been so beautiful, absolutely glowing! At the end of that aisle, they had said the most lovely vows to each other. He vowed to love and cherish her for all their days. He would take care of her always and he would let her take care of him. They were a team, so much in love, when he vowed forever, he thought one day he might be sitting outside the pearly gates waiting for her because he meant it.

Still, they kept moving forward, to election day, he watched his entire campaign with his wife by his side! They paraded, knocked on doors, kissed babies, the whole nine yards. No expense was spared, and even though he was a man of little words, he got his message across beautifully. He was a man for the people, who had grown up beside them and wanted to make a difference in their lives! People loved him everywhere he went!

Eventually, they moved on to the saddest moment in his life. They came upon a hospital room; his wife had been diagnosed with stage 4 cancer. All the happy moments that they had shared together played before his eyes, her learning the violin and making that awful screeching sound at all hours! Her painting her toenails and singing old show tunes. Talking all night long instead of sleeping. She was his best friend, and he couldn't imagine his life without her! Yet, it was here in this room that she stayed, and he had to move on.

He watched the rest of his big life moments with tears in his eyes; being reelected for mayor for another term, adopting his parakeet and cat, attending parties for work and family. Finally with memories run out they walked along in silence for some time. Until they happened upon a gate in the distance with a bench out front. On this bench sat his wife, "took you long enough" was all she could get out as he scooped her up in his arms vowing to never let her go again. They walked through the gates together as the reel faded to black.

She sat in her seat crying as applause erupted around her. The whole auditorium stood and clapped and huzzah'ed for Zarian's reunion with his wife. There wasn't a dry face in the crowd! *This*, she thought, *will be a worldwide sensation.* As she left the theatre others were asking about the reel, having heard the commotion there was interest in something that could spread hope instead of despair. Adrien decided to skip the next reel and go home, she had been to enough reels this week and she realized that she hadn't really been living her life anymore.

When was the last time she ate, or listened to music, or talked to a friend? She couldn't remember, it must have been before her father's passing. She had been worried about her mother; had she really been taking care of herself? She let these questions plague her as she settled down on the couch with a book.

# CHAPTER SEVEN

Adrien slept late for the first time that week, she awoke on the couch to the sound of her coffee machine beeping. Her book had slid onto the floor beside her, she picked it up and shelved it. She poured her coffee into her favorite mug, it was one she had stolen from home when she moved out on her own, the one her father had used whenever he wanted to keep her mother near while she was away. Adding cream and sugar she sat back on the couch and thought about her father, smiling for the first time that week, enjoying her coffee while it was fresh and hot.

*Ben was home, in the town where he had fallen in love, gotten married, and raised his three children. The town where he had served his people, helping all he could to build the lives, and afterlives, of their dreams. It seemed he was being granted one last day, the streets were empty, and there were no memories playing around each corner. He was being given the chance to say goodbye to the town that had raised him.*

*He walked to the end of the street, looking back one last time at his house, he continued to main street. This was where a little* shop stood tucked in between a florist's shop and a dental office. He used to joke with the dentist about people being closer to God after a filling than after a Sunday sermon. He walked past his shop sparing only a glance as he continued through town. On the far end started the farmland, this is where he would take his wife to pick her own flowers in the spring, and his children to pick pumpkins for Halloween in the fall. He knew the farmer well and had helped him decide what he wanted to spend his afterlife doing; the farmer had wanted to remain a farmer and look after all the animals that he had lost over the years. Still, Ben continued, on the other side of this farm was the town cemetery, he had attended many services here for friends and family. It seemed today he could watch his own, see that he was loved by many, although he couldn't hear a word they were saying, he knew it was a beautiful service.

"Would you like to say some last words to your family?" The Narrator asked.

"May I?" Asked Ben. The narrator motioned him towards the empty podium beyond his grave. He took his place and looked out at his family as they watched shovelfuls of dirt fall upon his coffin. "My dearest family, Sarah, my beautiful wife. My children, Ben jr, Katie-bear, and my sweet – not so little anymore – Adrien. You're all grown now, and into such amazing human beings! I couldn't have asked for three better children. I wish I had known the way I was going to miss the small things most. Benny, do you remember when we would put you to bed? As soon as we shut our bedroom door, you would sneak out of your room and drag a chair across the kitchen floor? We knew you were sneaking cookies after bedtime because that chair screeched the whole way, and you would stop halfway and say "Shhhh chair, we gotta be quiet!" in the loudest *whisper. We giggled in bed as we heard you push that chair back to the table on your way back to bed. You have grown into a kind and generous adult! Just know, your wife told us you still sneak cookies after bedtime, only now you're better at the sneaking part! Ben chuckled a little while wiping a tear from his eyes. My sweet Adrien, you would wake us up in the middle of the night because you kept having nightmares. I always wanted to be the one to banish the nightmares from your head, but all I could do was give you cuddles and no less than 15 kisses. Three on your nose, three on your forehead, three on your chin, and three on each cheek. If ever I stopped and told you I had given you all of them, you would say "No Daddy, that was only a couple, I need 'em all to go back to sleep" and make me start all over. Even when the nightmares ended, I would come into your room and make sure you were sleeping safely. You are such a brave and kind soul. Katie-bear, always my big girl, even when you were the littlest member of our family. You always made me proud! I felt like my heart would burst out of my chest when you would sit in my lap and read me the books you loved. Even before you knew how to read, you would bring a book and just babble at me. After a while, you would recite books you had memorized, even if you were holding the book upside down, I always made sure you knew you were doing a great job! Then as you got older, no matter how much you struggled with a word, you never wanted help sounding it out; you were determined to do it yourself! You are so brilliant sweetheart! I hope you never forget that. You three were our world, our everything. I love you more than I have words to express. It is because of you that I had the strength to face life, and now in death is it because of you that I have the strength to see this through to the end. Without your love and support, I would've never been able to walk through that first door. You've given me more than a father could ever ask for. I never wanted to say goodbye, I never wanted to leave any of you behind, but where I am going, though I do not fully comprehend, you cannot follow. Not yet. I love you all, take care of your mother for me. My sweet, sweet Sarah, if there is more beyond this, I'll be waiting for the day that we can be together again."*

Adrien finished her coffee, smiling as she let this memory fade. She was going to run errands today. She had been neglecting her home and needed to pick up some food and supplies from the local store. She called her mother and promised that she would stay away from the theatres, asking if she needed anything since she would be out and about. Her mother asked for a bottle of aspirin and a grapefruit soda, her favorite.

Adrien left on her bicycle, she had a basket large enough for some groceries and felt the need to stretch her legs and feel something in her body other than sorrow and confusion. As she pumped her legs on the pedals, she felt the stiffness in her legs start to ease and her heart felt light at the exertion. She felt alive in this one simple act and was so grateful to have had the idea to ride into town today. She passed the theatres on her way to the store, stealing a glance at the headlines in Hell: Addisyn Aimsley - Suicide, Jasmine Terga - car accident, and a worldwide sensation Jason Mallon - Untreated Rabies.

She took her time at the store, perusing the aisles with no direction, in no hurry, looking at the deals of the day. She was deciding between name-brand or off-brand cereal. She only needed a small amount because she didn't usually eat breakfast and at such a small amount the prices were comparable. She decided on a name brand, as the marshmallows tasted better in her opinion. She placed them in her basket with a 6 pack of eggs, a small bag of sugar and flour, a loaf of French bread, pasta noodles, and a half-gallon of milk. On her way to the check-out, she grabbed the grapefruit soda and a bottle of aspirin.

She dropped her groceries at home, then headed to her mother's house on foot. The weather was beautiful, birds were singing, and all the flowers were in bloom. She couldn't help but feel a little better. She stopped on the way to grab lunch for the two of them. They visited, having lunch in her mother's garden, recalling stories of Ben and his toiling away to make this garden such a beautiful place for the two of them. They shared some tear-filled hugs before Adrien headed back home, feeling hopeful that their grief was nearing an end.

Wandering home lost in thought Adrien missed her turn and ended up in front of the theatres. *Ok*, she thought, *I guess this is where I need to be.* She walked up to Hell and not wanting to witness the last day of the Rabies disease Adrien chose to attend Addisyn's death-reel.

"Ladies and Gentlemen... Addisyn Aimsley was a much-beloved daughter and sister; she leaves behind a mother and a younger sister. She lived alone, as alone was the way she liked to be, sadly no one could know how lonely she felt in her self-imposed isolation." The announcer's voice fell away in that familiar way that Adrien had begun to recognize.

Addisyn's reel started with her standing on a ledge. No build-up, no life flashing before her eyes, just this decision, the decision to fly. She stepped off and the crowd watched her fall, hair flailing behind her until she hit the ground and her spirit bounced out of her body. She stood and turned to look at her body lying on the sidewalk, a crowd starting to gather and sirens playing in the distance.

"Finally." She exclaimed softly, a look of peace spreading over her once-pained face. Taking stock of her surroundings she headed out into the town that she had once called home. She was from a big city, the hustle and bustle of city life was just right for her, she loved her apartment building and cherished her walks downtown, people-watching along the way. She walked down familiar streets until she came upon a pub, the crowd greeted her at the door, and she helped herself to a mug of her favorite draft, no matter how much she drank her mug never emptied. She stayed well into the night, listening to stories and watching the crowd she had grown fond of over the years getting rowdy and singing bar shanties. She smiled from her seat, put down her mug and headed towards the door. She headed for the park; she had always wanted to see it lit up at night but was always too afraid of running into trouble there in the late hours. She walked aimlessly under the streetlights taking in the sights, the park looked so different in the middle of the night, so peaceful. It matched the look on her face, complete peace. Along came a dog from the distance, running straight towards her.

"Abbie?" She asked as the dog jumped up to lick her face. "Abbie! I can't believe it's you!" She cried but no tears left her eyes, she stayed in the park with her childhood dog - long since gone - reunited again. She and Abbie headed towards home, she wanted to see her mother and her sister once more. She walked through the front door and sat at the dining room table talking to Abbie through the night waiting for her family to wake up and come to breakfast. She sat at the table silently watching them eat while thanking her mind for this last goodbye. She loved her family dearly and wanted to see them happy one last time. A phone rang in the other room, and her mother got up to answer it.

"Be strong for her" she whispered to her little sister who continued eating not noticing her sister's spirit. Then she got up and headed towards a door in the back of the room, it was slightly glowing, calling her to it. She turned the handle, took one last glimpse at the life she was leaving behind, a look of pained serenity on her face, and she stepped through pulling the door closed behind her. The theatre screen faded to black.

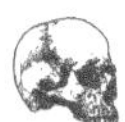

It was dark when Adrien left the theatre, she walked home under the streetlamps thinking of the jumper and the feeling of peace that she had with her decision. She thought of how selfish she thought the act of suicide was, knowing that the mother and little sister would suffer because of this. Then thought that maybe, in this case, the death reel would be a comfort for them both. Maybe that was the reason for the death reel after all, not to chronicle the last thoughts of the dying, but to comfort those who are left behind.

70

# CHAPTER EIGHT

It was 4 am again, Adrien had woken from a nightmare. None of it had made any sense. She ran snippets of the dream through her mind, a bottle of pills spilled across a bathroom floor, running water that never ended, and a sense of sadness that consumed her, it filled the room like a mist, suffocating her. Panting, she made her way to the bathroom. Nothing seemed out of place, she did what the sound of endless running water made the body do.

She headed back towards bed, glanced at it, decided not to tempt Mr. Sandman again, and went to her coffee pot. This morning she drank her coffee black, the bitterness combating the bitterness within her. She let the dark liquid warm her body and soul before starting her day. She picked back up the memory of her father's last words and the edges of her morning started to soften as she remembered him.

*After Ben finished addressing his family, he had tears streaming down his face. He thanked the Narrator for allowing him this last goodbye. The Narrator led Ben away from the podium pointing back in the direction of town and sent Ben towards the theatres. When he approached them, he could see bright signs on each building telling of his death. Both Heaven and Hell with their own spin on his death-reel poster. Below the lights was a door on each building, on the brighter building the door was labeled Heaven, and on the other, the door was labeled Unknown.*

*"What'll it be? Are you ready to say goodbye?" Asked the Narrator. Ben stood motionless looking from one door to the other, then he slowly stepped forward, opened a door, and stepped through into the Unknown once more.*

Heaven or Hell today? She flipped a coin, Hell it was. She headed towards the theatres. She had decided to visit Jason Mallon's death reel today. Curiosity had gotten the better of her and she wanted to know how such a horrific death would affect the reel. She bought herself breakfast at her favorite coffee place along the way and finished it before reaching the theatres. She bought a ticket for the first showing of the day.

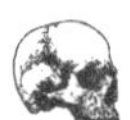

"Ladies and Gentlemen... Jason Mallon was an avid outdoorsman! He loved to hunt and fish and camp with family and friends. His favorite place to visit had been Honey Creek, Missouri. If you ever get the chance to go out there do think of him. He is survived by three rambunctious children, 5,7, and 8 years of age, a loving and devoted wife, Deborah, and a brother, Samuel. He will be missed sorely by all who knew him, there is a fund set up through the theatres to help provide for his wife and children if you feel so inclined to donate. All proceeds from his reel will be donated to the family."

Jason was running through the woods after his dogs, his brother at his side, hunting rifle grasped in both hands. He felt a sharp sting on his ankle but didn't think to look for the source, it was normal to get caught on debris in the woods. If you don't watch your footing, you can get a lot worse than a little scrape. Something had set the dogs off, the brothers tried to get them wrangled but weren't able to catch up for at least a mile. By the time they did, the dogs had lost track of whatever had excited them and lay in a clearing taking in the sun. Cursing to himself Jason knelt to check his ankle, he was bleeding, but it wasn't too bad. He took out his first aid kid and treated his wound, washing it out with an alcohol wipe and wrapping it with gauze.

"Damned Dogs," he muttered under his breath, but then his pup came over and licked his face, knocking him on his rear and he couldn't help but smile and laugh as the other dogs joined in; a doggy pile of sloppy kisses.

He and his brother had a great weekend hunting and playing with the dogs. When he got home his ankle had become itchy, but that didn't surprise him, itching was a sign of healing. It had scabbed over and was looking better every day. Exhausted from the long weekend, he kissed his wife and headed to bed. When he awoke the next morning, he had a mild fever. She was worried about him, but he didn't let it stop him from heading out to work. Over the next few days, his fever got worse, and he grew tired and nauseous. His wife took him to urgent care because she was worried. The doctors told them he probably had the flu and needed to spend some time in bed getting better. No one mentioned the cut on his ankle, why would they, it had already healed leaving behind an inconsequential, yet itchy scar.

As the week passed, his symptoms didn't ease. They were subtle at first, he would catch his wife looking in at him and wonder who she was, and why she was there. He got more and more confused about why he was in bed and whose bed was this anyway. He began to believe that this strange woman, "his wife" was trying to kill him. He took the first opportunity he had to escape the house. Outside the sun was blinding, his eyes wouldn't adjust no matter how he attempted to shade or cover them. The terrain looked foreign and the noise, oh the noise, where was that coming from? That was enough to drive a man mad! He ran as fast as he could to get away from the sound that he couldn't quite recognize as traffic.

He was captured by local law enforcement in the woods, but he wouldn't give in without a fight. He was taken to the closest hospital where he was restrained to his bed. He would scream and thrash when water was brought to him to drink. He continuously fought to rip the iv from his arm, believing that he was being poisoned. He fell into a coma, and never woke up.

As his body lay restrained in the hospital bed - flatline shown across the monitor above him - the audience held their breath, waiting for his spirit to arise, but it never did. He remained in his dead body, trapped. His consciousness screamed out as they placed him into a body bag and took him to the funeral home. An autopsy was performed on his body to find the cause of his death, Rabies had been the official diagnosis. He was embalmed at the request of his family because they wanted to have an open casket service for his memorial. His spirit silently screaming out as they dressed his body in his best clothes and laid him in his coffin. From within the coffin, he listened to his eulogy and heard everyone's last goodbyes as they viewed his face for the last time. He let out a silent sob as they lowered the lid of the coffin and lowered him into the ground. His spirit sobbed helplessly as he heard shovel after shovel of dirt thrown against the lid of his coffin. Until there was no more sound. Only darkness, only him, stuck in this decaying body. Time in the theatre sped up, but for him, he spent an eternity underground, the sound of bugs crawling in to feast on his flesh driving him ever more mad. His shell of a body slowly decayed in the coffin until all that was left was his consciousness, stuck forever in the ground under a headstone that read 'Loving Husband and Father, flies with the angels too soon!' The theatre faded to black.

Adrien felt sick to her stomach. How had this become a worldwide sensation? How could people watch this!? She decided it would be safest to ask to be cremated in her will, so that if this were her fate, her consciousness could be scattered to the earth and taken as far as the wind would allow.

This would be her last trip to the theatres, she had decided that today was the last day, it didn't matter how people died or what their afterlives were, her morbid curiosity had run its course. She headed home satisfied with her resolve and ready to face the world again tomorrow. When she got home, she saw a flashing light on her answering machine. Not having expected a call, she let it sit, content to check it in the morning. She was tired physically and emotionally and couldn't stand any more excitement for one day.

# CHAPTER NINE

4 am. She woke and headed to the kitchen, finally feeling an ease that she hadn't felt in over a week. Content with her decision to not go to the theatres anymore. She didn't need to know what others believed to make up her own mind about death. Heading for her coffee pot she poured herself a mug and began to walk to the table when she saw a flashing light in the hall. *Oh yeah,* she thought, *I have a voicemail.* Coffee in hand she headed for the box and pressed the button next to the flashing light.

"Hello is this, Adrien Burnum? Sarah Burnum's daughter? This is Alexington Hospital, I'm afraid we have some news regarding your mother, if you could give us a call back at..." The mug dropped from Adrien's hands, spilling coffee across her hallway as it fell onto her slippered foot. She immediately grabbed the phone and started dialing the number provided. *Everything's ok, everything's all right,* she mumbled to herself as she heard the ringing on the other end of the line.

"Hello?" a pleasant voice answered on the other end, "Alexington Hospital, how may I direct your call?" Adrien's voice caught in her throat. She choked back the tears that were threatening to fall and answered.

"Uh-hi, (clears throat) my name is Adrien Burnum, I received a voicemail about my mother Sarah Burnum? Is she alright? Where is she? Can I see her?" Her thoughts were racing as fast as her mouth was spouting questions. The operator, not being able to get a word in transferred the call directly to the doctor.

"Hello, Adrien? Am I speaking to Adrien Burnum?" He said in a solemn tone.

"Yes," she choked out, the tears she had been fighting slipping down her cheeks.

"I'm afraid I have some bad news regarding your mother. She was brought in here last night on suspicion of a drug overdose. We were unable to revive her. She slipped into a coma and passed in the middle of the night. I am so sorry for your loss. If you would like to get in touch with our grief counselor, we have one on staff for you to talk to, and the funeral director has already prepared her reel and her body. All we need from you is a couple of signatures when you're ready to come in." Adrien dropped the phone and crumpled onto the floor into a mess of tears.

She stayed like this, a mess of tears and snot, on the floor, listening to the dial tone of the phone hanging off the receiver. A drug overdose, she thought, why would her mother have suffered a drug overdose? She didn't have a drug problem; she barely took aspirin for her headaches. She needed to call her siblings and let them know. She would eventually have to stand up and face a world without her mother in it. How would she ever be able to face a world without her mother in it?

When she peeled herself off the floor, tears still flowing from her stinging eyes, it was 4 in the afternoon. She had drifted in and out of consciousness wondering if the phone call had been a bad dream, replaying the voicemail to confirm that it wasn't. She called her siblings and broke the news to them through sobs, they reacted the same as she had, disbelief and sorrow. Adrien walked to her room and lay in her bed, unable to face any more of this day. Maybe tomorrow she could go to the hospital and sign the paperwork. Maybe tomorrow she could face a world without her mom in it, but today she couldn't. She wrapped up in her favorite blanket and sobbed herself to sleep. She resigned to check in with her siblings in the morning, if she could make it out of bed to the phone.

The next day she woke up late. The coffee pot had stopped beeping long ago, but she had refused to get out of bed. Her eyes were swollen and painful, dried out of all the tears she had available. She got up still wrapped in her blanket and went to call her siblings. They agreed to go sign the paperwork together today, and tomorrow they would meet at the theatre to watch their mom's reel. They needed to know what had happened. Adrien got dressed and headed out on foot, her eyes were too puffy to drive. The walk would do her body good, she had drifted into a numb feeling and needed to wake up. Her heart pounded in her chest and tears threatened to fall as a light wind brushed her face, but she felt disconnected from it all. What did it matter if her heart was beating, when her mothers had stopped?

At the hospital, she gave the information desk her name and then waited for her siblings to join her. They were given paperwork to sign and given the contact information for the grief counselor. The staff was worried about Adrien's disconnected stare, she was not really there. They took the information and left. Adrien headed straight home, straight to bed. With her head on her pillow she looked at the glowing constellations on her ceiling and let her mind wander. How would she handle going to see her mother's reel? Would it be anything like her father's? Would she leave the theatre with more questions? How could her mother leave her children like this? Was it selfish that she didn't want her to go? Was it an accident? Was it on purpose? She drifted off to an empty sleep, devoid of dreams, just peaceful nothingness.

"Ladies and Gentlemen... Welcome to the death reel of Sarah Burnum. She was a mother of three who recently lost her husband. You could say she died of a broken heart." The death reel started as the lights in the theatre dimmed, Adrien sat next to her siblings, and they all held hands. Sarah was lying in bed crying. She got up because she heard the phone ring, it was her daughter checking in on her. They stayed on the phone for quite a while, not talking, just being together. Sarah laid back in bed with the phone beside her on speaker. She fell asleep like this. Later in the day, her daughter came to visit, she had brought some aspirin, and she was thankful because her head had hurt. They ate lunch and visited; it was the first day she had felt anything but sad since Ben had passed.

When her daughter went home, she got out her blender and some tequila. She filled the blender with tequila, margarita mix, ice, and half the bottle of aspirin hitting blend. She poured herself a glass and downed it, then poured herself another to enjoy. She put on some music in the kitchen, not too loud, and she danced, no care to the sink full of dirty dishes, sipping the drink in her hand. She danced until her drink was gone, then she went to bed with a photo of Ben beside her. She laid there drunk and peaceful, drifting into an eternal sleep.

Ben stood beside her bed, he reached for her hand, pulled her spirit from her body, and embraced her.

"You aren't supposed to be here yet!" He said.

"I couldn't wait," was all she could say. He smiled at her, she looked up into his eyes, the look on her face was peaceful. She was exactly where she needed to be. He led her to a door labeled Unknown, they both looked back towards the audience and nodded, then walked through. The screen faded to black.

As quickly as it had started it ended. Adrien's siblings wrapped her in a big hug as she sobbed. They knew what she was thinking, but there was no way this could've been prevented. They stayed like that for a while, in the empty theatre. Their mother's showing had only been thirty minutes, but it had left an impact that would last a lifetime. They eventually went their separate ways, heading home. When Adrien made it to bed, she cried herself to sleep, she wasn't sure she ever wanted to get back out of bed again.

# CHAPTER TEN

Adrien didn't know how long she had slept, minutes, hours, or days. She awoke refreshed, she thought of her mother holding her father's hand and breathed out a sigh. How could she be mad at her for leaving when she was exactly where she wanted to be? She got out of bed and set her coffee pot to run while she showered.

She went out for breakfast with her siblings. They had all needed an excuse to get out of the house, and after losing their parents they promised to check in often and remember that if they had each other, they were never truly alone. None of them thought about the theatres again, what lay beyond the grave didn't matter if they were truly living in the present; Whether it's all in their minds or there's room for the unknown is the last mystery life has to offer.

*Ben was back in the emptiness, surrounded by nothingness. He looked around him but there was nothing to see. Standing beside him was the narrator, looking expectantly at him.*

*"Is that it?" Ben asked.*

*"That's for you to decide." Replied the narrator. He waved his hands through the emptiness creating ripples in the open space. Ben stared at him in disbelief. "All this time you thought that you would get to choose," the narrator continued. "You thought that this was it, just a dream at the end, then lights out and nothing more. Yet as you stand in this nothingness, you can feel the unknown in the air around you. You can feel the endless possibilities that are waiting for you to discover them. Humans! How silly to believe that one person could know everything, sometimes it's best to trust in the unknown. You will get to decide if this is where your story ends, or if Benjamin Burnum has more beyond the grave."*

*As the narrator talked a door appeared beside them, this door was labeled After Life. Ben grabbed the handle, turned his head towards the audience, and said, "There is more beyond this." He winked and opened the door, the big screen faded, and the room was silent.*

Adrien had wondered if this was indeed her father's last lesson, a teacher, and an advocate, even in death. She thought about those words as she worked through her grief, she thought about those words as she attended every death reel that week. Maybe, we don't know what lies beyond. Maybe, we are all right, and maybe, there is room for more than one belief.

Maybe, there is more beyond this.

# AFTERWARD

"Ladies and gentlemen... Adrien Burnum Craigsly was a beloved wife and mother. Her children have asked that we read the eulogy that they have prepared: She leaves behind four children, twelve grandchildren, and her rescue dog Max. She spent her life inspiring others to live in the present moment, she believed that if we keep worrying about tomorrow, we will miss the joy that today has to offer! She and her husband were volunteers at their local shelter, taking joy in caring for the animals, even giving a few of them homes! She was inspired by her parents to always move forward and pursue truth, beauty, and justice. She was ready to go when her time came, saying, 'Death is life's greatest mystery.' She was loved, and she will be missed." The announcer's voice dropped off as the screen lit up.

Lying in bed was an elderly woman, she was surrounded by solemn faces, but she was smiling. She looked around the room at her family and sighed, this life had been everything she had ever wanted, and so much more. She took a long raspy breath and closed her eyes. Her spirit sat up out of her body, she took her time getting out of bed. She made sure to say goodbye to her grieving family one last time before leaving the room. Outside there was a man waiting for her.

"Narrator?" She asked. He nodded and took her hand. They walked together for a long time until they reached a door with no label. She knocked on the door, wondering what awaited her. Her mother and father opened the door, they embraced her. Tears were flowing between the three of them, no one wanting to let go. After a while, they welcomed her inside. Their home was magnificent! They guided her through the house, up a staircase, and down a hallway to a room labeled Adrien. She glanced at them once more before going inside. She inspected the room, there was a beautiful bed, an armoire, a desk for writing, and what looked to be a closet door. Upon further inspection the door had a label, it said Unknown. A smile spread across her face as she gripped the doorknob. Adrien turned to look at the room one last time, she was facing the audience, she winked and walked through the door.

# ABOUT THE AUTHOR

Hello! I thought I could use this as more of a get to know me and less of an autobiographical blurb. My name is Kimberly, as you can see on the front cover, but my family calls me Kiki. I have a wonderfully supportive fiancé who was the first to read this novella and tell me I should publish! We have two almost grown children, and an adorable nephew, they each hold a piece of my heart! My mom has been hounding me for years to write a book. So, here you go Mom, sorry about the content! And my Best-est friend has supported me through every write, and rewrite, and rewrite... She will continue to support me until we are both ghosts and then we will be ghost friends, forever! I love to travel, I have visited Paris France, Vancouver Canada, and have been to 13 of the 50 United States. My favorite color is yellow; it makes me smile every time I see a yellow canopy on a tree. Given that information you may have already guessed that autumn is my favorite season. Although, I am lucky enough to live in Oregon where I get to experience four distinct seasons! I've received my BS in Science at Portland State University. I am currently taking a break from any further academic pursuits to focus on my passions which include singing, writing, and quality time with loved ones.

I do not have a religious affiliation; I identify as an omnist.